# POSSESSION IS NINE-TENTHS

## J DARK

Published by Water Dragon Publishing
*waterdragonpublishing.com*

An imprint of Paper Angel Press
*paperangelpress.com*

ISBN 978-1-957146-10-2 (Trade Paperback)

FIRST EDITION

10 9 8 7 6 5 4 3 2 1

# AUTHOR'S NOTE

This particular tale came about after watching the movie *Constantine*. The opening scene portrayed the possession of a young girl by a demon. I asked myself: Why is it just people? Can't animals be possessed too? The result of answering those questions is what you see here.

As always, it isn't just one person that creates a story or book. There's the writer, editor, publisher, readers with comments. Without any of these people and their suggestions and encouragement, this story would never have been published. So thank you everyone. We made a fun story.

# POSSESSION
# IS NINE-TENTHS

T HE DAY INVADED MY PERSONAL SPACE with a gradual lightening of the comforting darkness. Next came the tortuous ringing of the bells on the alarm clock. That vicious little thing has it in for me. I tried to burrow deeper into the warm coverings and ignore the cutesy venomous ringing that threatened to drive a spike in my ears. Ten agonizing seconds later I finally started my day — by bringing my clenched fist down on the offending noisemaker. Irritated strength overpowered the small mechanical brass contraption, and the satisfying 'crunch' of flattening metal gave way to irritation. I was going to have to get another alarm.

Blessed sleep ran whimpering from the growing brightness and I sat up in bed, stretching my arms towards the ceiling and trying to keep them between me and the way too cheerful sunlight streaming in through the blue lace curtains on the floor-to-ceiling patio window.

Each morning can be an adventure. This morning I wake up after crunching the alarm, stretch, try to cover my eyes, and then turn and put my feet on the floor, only to find that the floor isn't there. The bed I'm in hangs in mid-air with no visible means of support, and my head barely avoiding a collision with the ceiling as my senses start to tell me things are very wrong.

The night stand drops from the side of the bed, falling to the floor with a splintering crash. My feet dangle off the edge and the bed tilts dangerously as reality and gravity grab me by the throat and give me a solid shake as a good morning greeting. The bed falls stopping just above the floor and gently settles. My feet touch the floorboards and flinch away. The wood was like ice. I look down and the floor is ice — at least a quarter-inch thick over the reddish cherry wood.

I stick my cold toes into bunny slippers as my breath hangs in the air as puffs of fog from my lips and grab my kimono bathrobe while my body complains that we should get some boiled brown bean juice (coffee, for the uninitiated) and see about getting my bra on and my hair untangled from the bird's nest it's in. Just another day of possession for yours truly.

You heard right. Possession. As in something not ready to pass on hides inside a person hoping that it can coerce whom it possesses into satisfying a last lingering regret or desire before it rejoins the choir invisible and moves on to its reward or whatever place restless spirits go. Fortunately for me, I'm not the one who's the possessed.

That would be my ferret, Imp. She's what is called a 'Siamese coated'. Her limbs are all a chocolate brown with a light tan body and a bandit mask. It's striking actually. Not as striking as her chatter when possessed. If you've ever heard a child try to squeak out curse words while trying to control an out-of-control object, you have a good idea of what it's like for Imp.

I inherited Imp from my grandmother years ago when she passed away. She'd been a medium of no small reputation, and Imp was the reason. I don't know how long ferrets live; the information online says five to seven years. Imp's been with me for eight, and was with my grandmother for at least eleven years that I can remember, which makes her a robust nineteen and still as frisky as a one-year old fuzzball. I wonder if the possession part has something to do with her long lifespan.

Imp has full control of her body, but the spirit can talk, usually screaming for the lovable little tube rat to slow down so they can talk to me and we can agree on a deal for their lingering business. After a negotiation of some mutually beneficial deal, we get about said business. Hey, stuff like this isn't for free. I have to make a living too. Otherwise I couldn't keep Imp in the style she's accustomed to.

Like today, she's sleeping on my bed, and came wide awake as it settled back to the floor. Her furry body launched off the bed onto the icy floor without a care in the world.

Me, even with the kimono on I shiver in real cold and check the thermometer on the wall by the patio door. It says -10C and that I'm welcome would I like to hear the forecast for today? I decline with ill grace. I'm never happy unless caffeinated. That being said, it was obvious that a spirit was in desperate straits to use Imp.

Obvious, you ask? Easy to answer. If you note I said the bed was floating in the air. I didn't suspend it from strings as a slight of hand trick. That's expensive and more effort than I want to put out for anything actually.

To answer the second unspoken question I know you're itching to ask: Why not me? Because I've no aptitude for psychic phenomena. Why a ferret has that kind of sensitivity is one of those things in the universe that no one has any idea. It just is. Imp was being her usual self, running to the food dish, finding it empty. Then realizing she hasn't done her morning ablutions, and runs for her toilet. Once that's done it's back to the food dish, then to me to ask if I could please hurry up and feed her since she's hungry thanks-ever-so-much?

I get there eventually, which is never fast enough, and get a scoop of ferret food for Imp. Then I can go about the real necessities, coffee for a wake-up, and eggs with bacon for me. Then I can get to the spirit in question. Said spirit was trying to talk around ferret crunchies and failing. Imp paid no attention to the funny noises while I waited patiently for her to finish eating and let the spirit communicate.

When Imp came over, I nodded at her, and she lay down in front of me, looking for all the world like a cat that had just claimed that spot for its own. I leaned over so the spirit could get a better look at me. Ferrets are notoriously near-sighted.

"Hello, I'm Kat Fox. Kat's short for Katheryn, and that's Imp. What can we do for you?"

Imp shifted lazily as the spirit tried to get a word in edgewise while she cleaned her belly fur.

"I'm ... ahh ... Chuck Wuerley." The spirit tried to gag as Imp started cleaning her butt. "Gah! Oh my god this is ... ack! What are you doing?! stop! Stop!" His discussion was put on hold while Imp finished her morning ritual. She looked back up at me and the spirit recovered enough control to resume talking.

"What is this? There's this weird taste in my mouth."

"That would be Imp's breakfast and some hair from her grooming. You're in a ferret, by the way, not a person."

The ferret continued to gaze up at me in what I suppose was stunned silence or ferrety satisfaction of a full belly and clean fur. You can never tell with spirits. Or ferrets. Some are okay with an animal possession. A few were ecstatic. Most are shocked and dismayed. Chuck seemed like the latter.

"A ferret? What the hell is a ferret?! I rolled my eyes and walked over to my bathroom. I had a mirror on the counter next to the sink, and picked it up. I walked back out to the still motionless ferret, and plunked the mirror down in front of her.

"It's a rat. I'm in a rat. Why am I in a rat?"

"Imp is a ferret, not a rat," I said indignantly. "Get your mammals straight, doofus." I waggled a finger right in front of Imp's nose as I spoke. Imp took this as an invitation to a play fight. She leapt up, dooking and shook her head side to side as she rapidly backed under the bed while the protesting Chuck tried to scream at Imp to stand still.

"Whoa! Stop! Stop! Dammit you little ass-wipe-fuzzy-stretch-rat stop! I need to talk the person. Stop dammit!"

Imp scrambled out from under the bed and pounced on my fingers, biting playfully at them as I flipped her over and tickled her belly.

"Waah ... ha ... hahahahaha! Stop! It tickles! Haaahahahah!"

Imp *dook*'d happily and flipped back over. She scrambled back under the bed, ran out, then ran back under again as I moved toward her. Chuck was pleading with me to stop and listen to him after another five minutes. I stopped playing with Imp, who made a few lunges and back-aways from me, then seeing playtime was over, noodled over to my feet and lay on her side.

"Okay Chuck. What's your situation besides being dead and all. What do you need to happen to go to the great beyond?"

"I want you to find my kid."

"Find your child? What happened? Did she run away? Or ...?"

"No no no no ... nothing like that. I want you to find my kid. My baby goat."

•　　•　　•

I couldn't help it. "Say ... what?"

"I need you to find my kid. That darn thing swallowed something that really needs to go back where it came from."

"Oh?" I raised my eyebrow. Both of them actually. I've done a lot of things, but, c'mon, a goat? And not just any old goat, a young goat. I've heard the old joke goats will eat anything from cans to car bumpers, but I never expected to be asked by a spirit to go find one. Chalk one up to spiritual diversity.

"Yeah, I know how it sounds. If I heard that I'd think the guy ... spirit ... had been sniffing something ... well not sniffing more like experienci..." he gave up looking for a good homily and went silent while Imp started cleaning herself.

"God that's weird. Does she do this all the time?" he asked with a fur muffled voice.

"Pretty much. Ferrets are very clean animals."

"Huh."

"So why do you need this baby goat found?"

"Because if it isn't found, things are going to get very bad."

"Better explain that one Chuck. That's not exactly helpful."

"I can do that, but you might want to sit down. A proper explanation is going to take a while. And if this tube rat starts going all hyper again it'll take longer."

"Hurry it up with the backstory, Chuck, she's going to sleep."

"I-got-hired-to-steal-a-seal-off-of-a-book-and-deliver-it-to-a-patron-The-book-was-a-prison-for-a-demon-and-it-possessed-my-client-It-will-get-its-power-if-it-isn't-sealed-back-in-the-book-The-seal-has-to-be-back-on-the-book-in-twelve-hours-or-the-demon-will-be-too-powerful-to-seal-I-tried-to-return-it-but-the-possessed-patron-killed-me-when-he-discovered-I-had-stolen-the-seal-back-He-came-to-my-farm-and-after-killing-me-he-walked-back-to-his-car-and-got-knocked-down-by-Doris-She's-the-mother-of-Tyke-who-swallowed-the-seal-and-ran-off-when-Bishop-Davis-tried-to-catch-him-He-ran-off-somewhere-and-time's-running-out."

I walked back over to my bed and sat on the edge. Imp curled her neck and nibbled at her flank then got up and trot-hopped, back arched over to lay down next to my foot.

"Shit."

"Yeah." Chauck said hollowly as Imp yawned.

Chuck seemed to clear his voice. I'm not quite sure because all I heard was a tired chirp from Imp.

"I … uh … was a specialist in procuring items difficult to acquire."

"In simple words you were a thief."

Chuck tried to sigh but ended up a burbling yawn from Imp. I wiggled the foot she was draped across to keep her awake. He started again as Imp chirped sleepily.

"Yeah, I was a thief. A good one. I'd do mostly old-style second story stuff. Break in, take a few valuables, and leave the same way I got in. People wouldn't even miss the stuff and it made me enough money to live comfortably after fences and the mob took their cuts for letting me work in their territory."

"And how does this information relate to … getting your goat?" I couldn't help it. Well, I could but I didn't want to. It was too good of a straight line. Besides, it was fun to hear the resigned sigh come from Imp.

"Keep your day job. Your timing sucks," he said petulantly.

I crossed my arms and stared down at Imp, and by extension, Chuck Wuerle. Chuck had just made a very vague, and ominous all-encompassing statement. Either he was exaggerating, or understating the problem. I was really hoping for the former.

I felt a huge mental breath as Imp yawned and fell asleep. That was lot to say. We had a threat, a demon, we had a name for the kid, Tyke, and an adversary, Father Davis. I could check church rolls online for both Father Davis and Chuck Wuerle. Or I could wait for Imp to wake up. As I pondered the next move my bed started floating again. I hopped off and watched it rise wobbily upward and bounce against the ceiling before dropping equally slowly to the floor. It landed with a thump, which woke Imp. She immediately surged under the bed with a sleepy 'dook!' and collapsed in a snoozing heap.

While Imp slept, I did some research on Bishop Davis. It took a while as church rosters aren't regularly updated, reason being it's a volunteer job to do so. Four hours later after the ninth or tenth search on churches, I finally found Bishop Davis. He was listed as the Leader of the local diocese and a part of the Haven Episcopal Church, which was located only about a forty minute drive south of Jackson on state Mississippi Highway 27, or the M-27 for you that like shorthand.

I kneeled down and scooped my sleeping medium from under the bed and put her in the pet carrier. Then Imp, Chuck the spirit, and I got in my Smart Car and toodled down M-27. You won't find Haven on any map of Mississippi, it's unincorporated and boasts only eighty-one residents. The town used to be a busy place during World War II. Saltpeter was processed here for shipment north to the munitions factories, and boasted about four thousand residents in its heyday.

It died out after the war and dwindled in number until five years ago it lost its status and was unincorporated.

The only large structure still in use was the Haven church in Copiah County.

•          •          •

I expected that the church would be easy to find, and it was, with signs pointing to the 'Historical Antebellum Haven Roman Catholic Church'. I was guided for the last ten miles by one placard a mile. They really wanted people to know where they were.

I turned off M-27 onto a dirt road that meandered lazily a few times before finally emptying into a small parking lot next to the church. There was only one other vehicle in the lot, which was a six-door Humvee in black paint with gold trim. It looked ostentatious, and honestly it was. But I suppose the bishop of a currently Episcopal formerly Roman Catholic Church felt that he had to be over-the-top to impress his flock in the wisdom of god and the angels. Yeah, I didn't believe me either.

The locusts, or Cicadas to you northerners, were shrieking up a storm from the stout and very old-looking magnolia trees that shaded the church. There was one at each corner of the small structure, and together they created a magical canopy of green over the building that was worth the trip alone.

Imp chose that moment to wake up like ferrets do, all at once, and noodled out the door at top speed, dooking and chirping like a little mad thing. Chuck was shouting something incoherent, I guess he wasn't a fast waker-upper like Imp. I strolled casually behind the hyperactive tube rat as she darted back and forth on the gravelly surface of the parking lot, daring me to chase her.

"Gah, stop! Please stop! I'm dizzy!" Chuck burbled drunkenly as the little bandit took off again, making a beeline for the parked monster at the far end of the lot. Imp playfully attacked the front tire as Chuck started complaining about the taste of rubber in between excited ferret noises. Personally, I'd really would have loved to dip Imp in ink and let her run wild inside the Humvee to see if she could coat everything in black before we had to go home. Yes, the car was an eyesore, and I was willing to bet the inside looked just as overpriced-tacky as the outside.

Imp finished her play attacks and darted back to me with a wiffling chirp. I've learned to interpret ferretese a small amount and the kind of noise means that whatever the spirit in her was looking for had been in that eyesore. 'Had been' being the important part. Having ascertained by ferret medium of the former location of the seal, and by her excited chirps that 'had been' was recent, I grabbed my wiggly little bundle of solid energy and dropped her in my shoulder bag and quickly zipped it shut.

Imp calmed down in the dark, and Chuck made some muffled noises which I chose to interpret "Hey! You're doing a great job, keep it up!", rather than as "Hey! What the H-E-double hockey sticks is going on let me outta here you fiend! Gah don't lick your butt! BLECH! Oh god I'm gonna be sick." I patted the bag gently and turned to the souvenir shop that was just to the east of the historic edifice.

The grey-haired woman behind the cashier counter looked up as the small bell mounted above the door tinkled. She gave me a broad smile that turned to puzzlement as I stepped to her while my purse made muffled pleas and retching sounds.

She stared at the bag until I cleared my throat politely.

"Yes, hon, can I help you?" Her eyes drifted to the purse which had started to pulse like a paper bag over a hyperventilating man's mouth. I have to admit the bulging and deflating as Imp shifted inside did seem kind of mesmerizing.

"I was wondering if you could direct me to Bishop Davis? I have a donation that was returned due to an improper address, so I've come by to place it in his hand." I paused, then added, "The donors would prefer for their peace of mind."

The lady, who was maybe five-foot even, and likely tilting the scale at what a nose tackle would, strode, waddled actually, from behind the desk.

"That's unusual, but I don't see the harm. The bishop has all sorts of donors to help maintain the church." She turned sideways through the front door, and began walking towards the church proper.

"The bishop is in his office at the back. He keeps the doors closed while he's working. It makes it easier for him to focus."

I nodded absently as we stopped at the front doors. She produced a key from the small fanny pack she wore, and pushed it into the slot. The magnetic locked popped quietly, and the door creaked open slightly. I smiled at her then pushed the door further and entered.

The church actually was worth the visit. It was small, but the high ceiling and the glowing honey-colored wood made it feel much larger. The walls were braced by columns about twelve feet apart that went straight up to the edge of the ceiling then bent, angling upwards in one solid piece to meet at the crown. Three or four feet below the crown lay a cross bracket of the same wood, so carefully fitted that it gave the feeling it grew out of the wood like some large branch, to link with the other roof beam and creating a whole frame from one piece of wood. The floor was only slightly darker than the beam and column, being a darker yellow-brown.

The whitewashed walls were a bright accessory that made the wood seem to glow from the sunlight coming through the stained glass at each end of the church, one above the door I came in, and one above and behind the pulpit which was centered on a small raised section of the floor at the back of the church. Needless to say, it was beautiful, but I will anyways. I had never seen that kind of craftsmanship before.

I was so entranced that I was surprised when Imp popped her head out of my purse chittering excitedly. A creak came from the right and towards the back of the church, where a thin gentleman in an expensive looking grey suit had just stepped through a door to the priest's alcove.

The acoustics were so good I could hear him mutter "My slacks are ruined! To think a goat that small had that much crap in his stoma ..." he chose that moment to look up when he heard Imp's chittering, which changed from excited dooking to a full-on weasel war cry. His head came up and he gaped openmouthed at me. Then everything shattered into motion.

Imp leapt from my bag and hit the ground, scrabbling madly on the smooth surface as she tried to reach Bishop Davis. It had to be him. Chuck was yelling "You! You! You!" as Imp ran in place on the slick floor.

I charged forward, trying to grab Imp before she reached the bishop. As a medium, my fuzzy little girl can feel the emotions of the dead and they influence her reactions. The stronger the emotion, the more she is affected. Chuck obviously, had a very big reaction to seeing his killer. Imp was fuzzed up tip to tail like she'd been plugged into a wall socket. The sight of her screaming at the bishop, and running madly in place trying to get to him was pretty comical for all the unfolding drama.

Bishop Davis gawked open-mouthed at the display of churning tiny feet under a fuzzy tubular body, then started to do a quick about-face and slipped on what looked like a small pile of mud that had peeled off his pants leg as he turned. He landed with a thump on the edge of the raised platform that held the pulpit and chairs for the choir.

Imp finally got traction and darted out from under my grasping hands, and did a high-speed noodle straight at the stunned bishop, who rolled onto his back and unsteadily attempted to sit up. She wriggled up his sleeve and the bishop started grunting and trying to slap his chest as Imp churned madly inside his jacket.

I sprinted for Bishop Davis. I didn't want him to smash Imp. The Imp-lump scooted into his armpit as I arrived and missed his hand just as Imp dashed around to his back and popped out of Davis's collar with a funny-looking roundish wooden thing in her teeth. She dropped to the floor as the bishop got his wits back and snarled at Imp. "Give that back!"

Sometimes the emotions of the spirit can muddle their desire, and said spirit goes crazy trying to get Imp to do what it thinks it wants. this happens more than I care to admit. However, there are times when both medium and spirit are in total agreement.

Both Imp and Chuck hated the bishop; Chuck because the man killed him and Imp because the bishop is a black practitioner. Yes, he used Black Magic. Something about magic that uses negative emotions like fear or channels emotions from violent things like death or torture create a kind of aura about the user. Animals hate and fear said person and do their best to put as much distance between them and the practitioner, except in certain psycho-ferret cases.

More importantly, Chuck knew what that wooden disc was and what would happen if it wasn't recovered, and that scared him more than his hate for Davis. Imp responded to his desperate need and had grabbed the seal from the bishop's pocket. I stepped past the bishop as he turned away from me to pursue Imp. As he started to rise, I kicked hard at his head and connected. The bishop dropped back to the floor with a hard thump. I did the same, clutching my leg. My ankle hurt like crazy.

Imp ambled across the floor to flop down on her side next to my feet, seal still in her mouth, churring impishly at me, blatantly asking for a belly rub.

"Oh god that thing tastes awful! Demon taste BLECCHHH!" Chuck's voice came from Imp. "He ... nnnng! ... fed the kid a purgative so it'd throw up the seal. Only he didn't realize everything would come out the other end." He paused to take a breather. "It's weird that he could shoot me without blinking an eye, then turn around and cringe at killing a goat."

"He probably didn't want to take a chance on ruining the seal by cutting it open" I answered after a few moments of thought. A seal is meant to keep things in or under control. Any damage and the seal's magic could blow up in your face, or worse, lead whatever it was that had been sealed to your door and in an infernally pissed off mood.

Chuck sighed, then Imp chirped lazily and fell asleep still holding the seal. I picked her up and tickled her belly enough to wake her and drop the seal. It was still covered in goat goo, so I wrapped it in my handkerchief, and stuck it in a side pocket of my shoulder purse. I didn't want to chance it rolling around loose in my handbag with a hyperkinetic ferret.

From there I could embellish the troubles getting the seal back and the horrific challenges we faced, but I would be lying through my teeth. It really was simple affair to call an ambulance for the bishop and the police.

Bishop Davis had started to revive when the police showed up, and it was a lively ten minutes to get them to listen to Chuck and arrest the bishop. I think what really sold them was the goat in the rectory and the explosive and fragrant redecoration of it. When I produced the seal as evidence, the bishop attacked the officers holding him and had to be tackled down by the cops. They put him under arrest and recorded Chuck's statement, once on a cellphone that didn't take (spirits can't be recorded), and the second by hand and signed by me, and the recording officer.

We went back to my apartment, where I let Imp noodle out of my purse onto the floor. Chuck told me the name and address of the person he'd stolen the seal from, and, after Imp and Chuck had once more fallen asleep, I put my medium in my purse and the three of us, manager, medium, and spirit drove out to the Bannick estate to return the seal.

Hazen Bannick, the wheelchair-bound portly white-haired long-faced prestigious religious scholar welcomed us into his home and had us stand by in his study while he set up a Circle of Solomon to replace the seal on the book. Said book was an eighteen by twenty-four inch bible with a cavity in its front cover which was the perfect size to hold the wooden object. After the seal was carefully washed in his sink of the wet bar to clean off the goat residue, Hazen rinsed the wood in holy water. Once it was dry, he stepped into the Circle of Solomon with book in his right hand and the seal in his left.

Chanting something I didn't understand, but I think was Hebrew, he placed the seal in the depression on the book. The seal settled into the cavity with a loud 'click' and a howl of rage from the demon as book and seal magically locked together, once more trapping it in its holy pages. I for one was very glad that we didn't have to do anything other than watch.

Hazen sent us home with thanks and a copy of his latest work, 'Infernal: Everyone needs Hell'. It's large and heavy enough to credibly pass for a boat anchor if by some odd emergency you needed one and this was in the boat with you.

"So ... umm ... now that my ... ahh ... business is finished ... what happens now?" Chuck asked me timidly.

I thought about giving him a smart mouth remark but held off. Unlike some previous spirits, he'd not tried to demand, wheedle, or coerce Imp and I in some fashion. He'd told us the problem and didn't try to get in the way. Even at the end, facing the man who killed him, Chuck worked with Imp, not against her. Imp liked him.

For a thief, she thought he was a pretty stand-up guy. Which is why he was still inside her. She'd have exorcised him from her fuzzy body the first moment his business was finished if he'd been coarse and demanding. Imp was allowing him the time to choose his moment to pass.

"So, uh ... do I just fade away? Is there a bright light? How does this work?"

I couldn't help it. I laughed, long and loud. Imp churred irritably and pounced on her dingle ball, which got a soft chuckle from Chuck.

When the laughter finally wound down, I said to him, "I don't know how it works. That's Imp's expertise. What I do know is that I don't know. I'm guessing it's a 'learn on the fly' sort of experience much like learning to walk or ride a bicycle is when you do it for the first time."

I felt rather than saw his nod. Imp simply lay on her side, dingle ball clutched in all four paws as she and Chuck gazed at me. Imp shifted and sneezed, then closed her eyes.

"I'm going now, thank you for helping me out."

"Good luck, Chuck" I said with a smirk. It got a last chuckle from him. "Yeah, good luck to you too, Ms Fox."

There was the faintest sigh like a low expelling of breath. Imp yawned then flopped asleep. She didn't snore but the little whistles as she slept were outrageously cute. Chuck was gone through the veil to whatever awaited him.

Imp and I would have a day or two of relative quiet until the next spirit could find us, or find her more accurately. Then things will get interesting again. In the meantime, I'm going to have to call the job line to see what I can get to make ends meet. The medium gig is a wonderful one, but like with Chuck, it doesn't pay bills. We can chat again later, but right now I have other things to take care of. See ya!

# ABOUT THE AUTHOR

J Dark is a latecomer to the writing profession, but enjoying every moment that life will allow. "The best thing to me is writing a story that someone enjoys. If I've made something fun and entertaining for people, it's a win-win."

J Dark lives with a house full of dreams, three cats, and various friends who occasionally drop by and stay for a while.

The author lives in Kansas, where the winds blow all the time, and, if you blink your eyes, the weather changes. You can find out more about the author's work at *The Pandemonium* (*thepandemonium.net*).

# ALSO BY THE AUTHOR

## HOT DROP

*What starts as a rescue mission in a combat zone on a hostile planet becomes something more.*

## THE JIMINY

*A man who had led a less-than-perfect life finds out that it's never too late for redemption.*

## SAYING GOODBYE

*A young girl, searching for the parents who abandoned her, discovers that some answers only lead to more questions.*

Available in paperback, digital and audio editions from
Water Dragon Publishing
*waterdragonpublishing.com*

# YOU MIGHT ALSO ENJOY

## THE ALCHEMIST DAUGHTER

by Paul S. Moore

*When a concoction of ethers channels a little of their magic properties to one location, inspiration springs to life.*

## PARRISH BLUE

by Vanessa MacLaren-Wray

*Sallie never expected to discover a world she'd forgotten how to imagine.*

## THE THIRD TIME'S THE CHARM

by Steven D. Brewer

*When an airship is hijacked by pirates, a young man with a secret loses his mentor ... and his future.*

Available in digital and trade paperback editions from
Water Dragon Publishing
*waterdragonpublishing.com*